The Fairy in the Kettle Gets Magical

PAULINE TAIT

Illustrated by Debbie Bellaby

Published in 2019 by SilverWood Books

SilverWood Books Ltd
14 Small Street, Bristol, BS1 1DE, United Kingdom
www.silverwoodbooks.co.uk

ISBN 978-1-78132-811-8 (paperback)
ISBN 978-1-78132-812-5 (ebook)

British Library Cataloguing in Publication Data
A CIP catalogue record for this book is available from the British Library

Page design and typesetting by SilverWood Books
Printed on responsibly sourced paper

SilverWood

Leona Rose awoke with a start!
Someone was knocking on the spout
of her precious kettle and shouting to
her to come quickly. The fairy elders had
called an urgent meeting and every fairy
in the glen had been ordered to attend.

Sleepily, Leona made her way to the elders' hollow in the giant beech tree. Her three best friends, Tilly, Robbie and Toby were waiting for her and, together, they listened as the elders reminded them about the pixies living in the swamplands on the outer edges of Bramble Glen.

The elders also told the fairies that, many years ago, the pixies would sneak into the fairy village and steal the fairies' precious fairy dust, using it to cause chaos and mischief throughout the glen.

So, the elders had decided that the only way to keep the fairies and the glen safe was to hide their fairy dust, keeping only enough for the elders to use in emergencies. This had kept the pixies away and the fairies had lived peacefully for many years. Now, however, their supply of fairy dust was running dangerously low!

Unfortunately, as so much time had passed, the secret of where their precious dust was hidden had been long forgotten. The elders needed all the fairies in the glen to come together and search for their dust before they ran out completely.

Leona and the older fairies could still remember fairy dust being used in the glen. They could remember its warm amber glow shimmering and sparkling as it danced through the air, twisting and turning as it went.

More importantly, they could
remember that the magic was not only in
the fairy dust itself — it was also in the fairies!
In every fairy! They knew that the fairy dust was only
needed to carry their magic wherever they needed it to go!

Listening to the elders, the younger fairies began to realise that they too had magic within them and excitement grew as they prepared to search the glen.

Leaving the elders' hollow behind, the fairies set off in search of the hidden fairy dust. Leona and her friends spent hours searching the glen. They searched the hollows of ancient trees, inside the old abandoned rabbit burrows and even under the horrible old anthills!

Eventually, tired and wondering where they could possibly look next, the fairies stopped to rest on the banks of Buttercup Brook. They chatted about what they would do if they couldn't find the dust, or worse, if someone or something else had already found it!

It wasn't long before the fairies began their search again. They were just leaving the brook when Leona glanced up at the waterfall tumbling down into Buttercup Brook. Suddenly, she noticed a small opening in the rocks about halfway up. Flying off for a closer look, she called to her friends to follow.

As they got closer they could see that the opening was much bigger than they had first thought. Desperate to explore, Leona and her friends went inside. The fairies were only a few steps in when they realised that they were standing at the entrance of a cave.

There was a strange musty smell and the sound of the water crashing over the rocks outside was like thunder. Slowly, they crept further into the cave, but the further in they went, the darker it got. They were going to need help — they were going to need the fireflies!

Leona, Tilly and Robbie waited
excitedly as Toby went to gather the
fireflies. It was their nap time and Leona
knew that they wouldn't take too kindly to
being disturbed in the middle of the day.
But, thankfully, Toby soon returned with
a swarm of grumpy fireflies following on behind!

So, with the fireflies lighting the way, the fairies flew deeper into the cave. It was long and winding and went deep into the hillside. The strange musty smell was getting stronger and there was a layer of thick, slimy moss covering the damp walls and floor.

Suddenly, everyone stopped. A warm amber glow was coming from the back of the cave and it wasn't the fireflies! Leona knew exactly what it was!

The glow was dancing and sparkling, twisting and turning in the air, just as she remembered. They had found it — they had found the fairy dust!

While Tilly and Toby rushed back to the village to gather the elders, Leona and Robbie flew further into the dazzling light and deeper into the cave.

The excited elders rushed to the entrance of the cave and, following the trail set by the fireflies, flew deeper and deeper into the darkness until they too were met by the sparkling amber glow. They could hardly believe their eyes — the cave went deep under Fairy Glen and it was full, full of
fairy dust!

Realising that their newly-found supply of fairy dust would be much safer staying in the cave, it was decided that the fairies would only take enough as could be safely hidden from the pixies.

The elders quickly set about giving each fairy their very own supply of fairy dust and, while they were still in the safety of the cave, the fairies were also given a lesson on how to use it!

As evening fell over Bramble Glen, the fairies returned to their village. They practised their newly-found magic well into the night and watched as the fairy dust danced and dazzled in the moonlight. It shimmered and sparkled, lighting up their beautiful village with its warm amber glow.

Exhausted, Leona and her friends returned to her kettle for some fresh spring water and berries. Magic had returned and, as the fairies celebrated into the night, they knew that life in Bramble Glen would never quite be the same again!

Praise for 'The Fairy in the Kettle'

"Everything is perfect, from the art to the plot to the words. One of the best children's books I've ever seen." — Paul Franco, NetGalley and Goodreads

"A story about differences and acceptance and living in harmony, this is, by far, one of the most wonderful children's books that I ever have read or reviewed." — Mackey S., NetGalley and Goodreads

Praise for 'The Fairy in the Kettle's Christmas Wish'

"Once again, Pauline Tait has given us a wonderful story of true friendship along with page after page of enrapturing illustrations. The story is enchanting, mesmerizing and delightfully told." — Mackey S., NetGalley and Goodreads

"Imaginative and engaging, highly mystical and whimsical story full of symbolism! Tait has truly created her own Christmastime Myth, which everyone can appreciate." — Gayle G., NetGalley

"The perfect bedtime story to send your little ones to sleep with dreams of magic and Christmas." — Dawn-Tracy B., NetGalley

Lightning Source UK Ltd.
Milton Keynes UK
UKHW051030300419
341829UK00002B/6/P